BOOMER THE ROO

The Little Aussie Adventure Book Collection

Here come the Little Aussies,
    One
            Two
                    Three.
Slipping and sliding down the old gum tree.

Kip the Koala has climbed down fast,
and here comes Smokey,
                Buttons is last.

It's holiday time and there's so much to do,
but first they must find their friend,
                Boomer the Roo.

Kooka and Squawk swoop in down from the sky
and an emu called Tangles,
　　　　who <u>does</u> want to fly.

"G'day Little Aussies! Now what's there to do?
The sunshine's so bright and we're on holidays too.
We'll all have lots of fun, but–
　　　　Where's Boomer the Roo?"

The koalas ride Tangles down the track to the sea
where friend Boomer the Life-saver takes morning tea.
But their wonderful white beach is totally bare.
The surf is fantastic,
                  But Boomer's not there.

So Kooka and Squawk fly way up in the blue,
to search for the hop-prints of the big kangaroo.

Now Kip is a surfer, and the water looks great,
so he jumps on his surfboard,
        'though he knows he should wait.
But "As I can ride Tangles," brags Kip the Koala,
"I can ride any big wave in Australia."

So out he goes over the waves without fear.
"Naughty Kip!" Buttons cries,
        "Wait 'til Boomer is here."

But silly Kip doesn't wait, and floats way out of sight,
while poor Smokey and Buttons start crying with fright.

Tall Tangles the Emu heaves a great big sad sigh,
for he knows he could save Kip,
        if only he could fly.
He looks out to sea and wonders what he can do.
Where are Kooka and Squawk?
        Where is Boomer the Roo?

Now what's all this noise, heading down to the sea?

Lots of laughing,
  noisy squawking,
    and Big Boomer's "Coo-ee."

Smokey and Buttons and Tangles start cheering,
as they watch the big roo down the sandhills careering.

"Great! We're all here together!"
booms the giant of Australia.

"But hold it – who's missing?
        Where's Kip the Koala?"

When Buttons tells Boomer that Kip's lost at sea,
he jumps on to "Roo-Power",
        his rescue surf-ski.

Kooka and Squawk fly off up and away.
They're the best spotter birds,
        "We'll find Kip," they say.

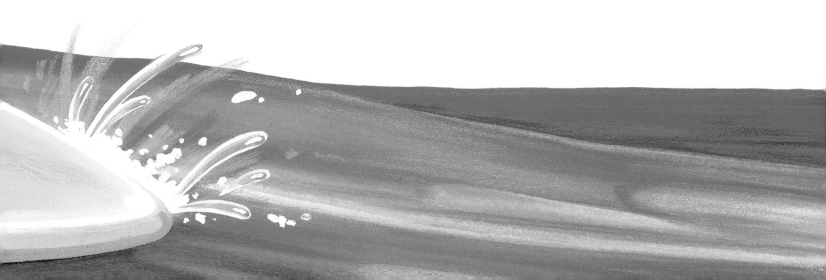

By now Kip is frightened, at sea all alone.

He's worried,
        he's wet,
                and he wants to go home.

Then Hooray! – here comes Boomer,
to tow Kip to shore,
where all the Little Aussies are smiling once more.

To swim out alone was a stupid thing to do.
"Don't you do that again, Kip!" warns Boomer the Roo.

"Well friends," drawls Tangles, "No more surfing today;
so if you'll all gather 'round I'll pour tea if I may."

They're all very happy as they sit in the sun,
    laughing
        and joking,
            and having great fun.

They're planning more adventures, exciting and new,
but in future they'll not go without –
        BOOMER THE ROO.